W9-AXO-439

DISCARD

MATHNET™ CASEBOOK

#5 The Case of the Mystery Weekend

By David D. Connell and Jim Thurman

Illustrated by Danny O'Leary

DISCARD

Scientific
BOOKS FOR YOUNG READERS
American

Children's Television Workshop

W. H. Freeman/New York

Copyright © 1995 Children's Television Workshop. **MATHNET** characters © 1995 Children's Television Workshop. *The Case of The Mystery Weekend* is a **Square One Television** book produced by Scientific American Books for Young Readers, in conjunction with Children's Television Workshop. Square One Television and **MATHNET** are trademarks and service marks of Children's Television Workshop. All rights reserved.

No part of this book may be reproduced by any mechanical, photographic, or electronic process, or in the form of a phonographic recording, nor may it be stored in a retrieval system, transmitted, or otherwise copied for public or private use, without the written permission of the publisher.

Scientific American Books for Young Readers
is an imprint of W.H. Freeman and Company,
41 Madison Avenue, New York, New York 10010

On **MATHNET**, the role of George Frankly is played by
Joe Howard; the role of Pat Tuesday is played by Toni Di Buono;
the role of Benny Pill is played by Barry K. Willerford; the role
of Sergeant Abruzzi is played by Michael Sergio; the role of
Captain Joe Grecco is played by Emilio Del Pozo.

Cover photo of Joe Howard and Toni Di Buono
© CTW/Richard Termine

Illustrated by Danny O'Leary

Activities illustrated by Sarah Albee

Library of Congress Cataloging-in-Publication Data

Connell, David D.

The Mystery Weekend: Mathnet Casebook/by David D. Connell and Jim Thurman.

p. cm.

Summary: Math detectives George Frankly and Pat Tuesday take a wrong turn going to a mystery weekend and come to a manor where they need their math skills to solve a real mystery.

ISBN 0-7167-6554-3 (hard).—ISBN 0-7167-6555-1 (soft)

[1. Mystery and detective stories.] I. Thurman, Jim. II. Title.

PZ7.C761853Cam 1995

[Fic]—dc20   94-1858
                                                                    CIP
                                                                    AC

Printed in the United States of America

10 9 8 7 6 5 4 3 2 1

CHAPTER
1

Pat Tuesday was feeling glum as she exited the subway to a gray and chilly New York City. It was Friday morning, and Pat found herself with no plans for a Fun City outing. *Maybe I'll frizz my hair, drink a couple of diet sodas, and do a load of clothes at the laundromat,* she thought, feeling sorry for herself.

Pat crossed Centre Street in lower Manhattan, narrowly avoiding two taxi cabs, three lawyers chasing an ambulance, and a pothole that looked deep enough to hold Olympic diving trials. Pat smiled ruefully, took a deep breath, and marched up the steps to Mathnet Headquarters. She picked up her messages from Sergeant Abruzzi in Dispatch and walked to her office.

"Some people get calls from Charlie Sheen or Tom Cruise," Pat muttered, glancing at her messages. "I get messages from my accountant about income tax and from my dry cleaner saying he's lost my blue silk dress. Oh, well, *c'est la vie.*"

But Pat's day took a turn for the weird the moment she opened her office door. There was a stranger sitting at her partner's desk. A very strange stranger. The man wore a caped coat and an old-fashioned tweed suit. A deerstalker hat sat on his head, with the hat's earflaps tied on top and a visor extending fore and aft. The man was concentrating on a brochure, studying it under a huge magnifying glass. He didn't seem to notice Pat's entry. Pat moved closer. That's when she noticed a familiar beaky nose poking out from under the hat.

"By George, it's George," Pat muttered, reaching out to touch his odd hat. "Nice lid, George. Are you coming or going?"

"Ack!" George jumped, startled. He looked up quickly, the magnifying glass still held close to his eye. An enormous eyeball glared at Pat.

"Ack!" She yelped in reply.

George recovered first. Affecting an English accent, he greeted his partner. "Good morning, Patricia." He leaned back in his chair and stuck a pipe in his mouth.

"I didn't know you played alto sax," Pat said, looking at the curved pipe. She sat down at her desk.

"Very funny, Pat. It's not a saxophone; it's a pipe. The kind Sherlock Holmes used to smoke in all those books and movies," George explained defensively.

Pat just nodded. She was busy checking out the rest of George's costume. "George, would you mind telling me why you're all gussied up this morning?"

Before George could answer, the telephone rang. George picked up the receiver. "Mathnet, Frankly. Oh, hi, Martha. . . ." He covered the mouthpiece and said to Pat, "It's Martha, my wife. I'm married to her."

"George, I've known your wife for years. Say hello for

me." Pat shook her head. George returned to his phone conversation.

"Pat says hello to you, Martha . . . claims she's known you for years. What? But Martha, I've been counting on this for weeks. How could you forget you had a final exam with the chef at the Cordon Bleu?" George sounded distressed. Even his earflaps drooped. "Why did you have to go to a cooking school in the first place? You cook plenty good already." There was a long pause. "Okay, I'll ask her."

George took the receiver from his ear and looked at Pat. "Can you be murdered this weekend?"

Pat stared at George, her mouth agape. He returned to the phone. "Just send the costume over, Martha. I can talk Pat into anything. I'll call you later, honey."

"You're going to talk me into being murdered?" Pat asked, as George replaced the receiver.

George nodded happily. "Martha wants to know if you can fill in for her, Pat. You don't have anything to do this weekend, do you?"

"Of course I have things to do this weekend, George Frankly," Pat responded, blushing at her white lie. "I'm always busy on weekends."

"Yeah, right," George said. "Like the time you went to that antique thimble exposition."

"It was very . . . interesting," Pat said, shuffling her phone messages.

"Or when you watched the supermarket checkout people give their Annual Poetry Reading and Bagging Concert," her partner continued. "Come on, Pat, come to a mystery weekend with me. It'll be great."

"Mystery weekend?" Pat perked up. "Is that where everybody plays a part and tries to solve a crime?"

"Correct, my dear Watson," George said in his best British accent. In his normal voice he rushed to explain. "It's all make-believe, and the crime might be a murder mystery or a kidnapping or a hidden treasure. And the location is terrific. It's held in a spooky old manor house called The Qualms in upstate New York, and I'm captain of the team. Will you do it, Pat, please?" George begged, dropping to one knee and clasping his hands together.

"You," Pat surmised, "will be Sherlock Holmes?"

George shook his head. "Sherlock *Condo*, Pat. It's

modern day."

"Who was Martha going as?" Pat asked. She took a stab. "Dr. Watson?"

"Dr. Whatzit."

"I should have guessed," Pat said, rolling her eyes.

"So will you go with me, Pat?" George pleaded, still kneeling. "Hurry up and decide; I'm getting a cramp."

"Well, I guess I can cancel a few things, make a few phone calls," Pat said, toyingly.

"Does that mean yes?" George demanded, struggling to his feet.

Pat gave in. It sounded better than a date with laundry detergent. "Yes. When should we leave?"

George smiled and scooped up a road map from his desk. "I was just going to figure that out. Let's look at the map."

George used his magnifying lens to enlarge his view of the map. "It's near the town of Bile, New York, just above Rising Gorge."

"How far is that from here?" Pat asked.

George placed a ruler next to the scale line on the map. "One half-inch equals twenty miles," he noted. He moved the ruler onto the map and placed one end of it at New York City.

Pat moved the other end near Bile. "Bile is about four inches from New York City."

"Four inches equals eight half-inches. At twenty miles per half-inch, eight times twenty is one hundred and sixty miles." George did some quick figuring. "At an average speed of fifty miles per hour, it should take us just about three hours."

"Yes, but look at the map," Pat said, tracing the route with her finger. "We can average fifty miles per hour on good highways, but we've got only three inches of those." Pat's finger left the highway and headed for some thin, squiggly lines. "That last inch looks like it represents some pretty questionable roads."

George nodded his head in agreement. "Three inches of good roads is one hundred and twenty miles, so that will take us about two and one-half hours. Then we have one inch, or forty miles, of bad roads. Maybe another hour or hour and a half?"

"Sure," Pat said. "Figure four hours total, tops."

"Okay," George said. "We are to be there at six p.m., so I'll pick you up at your place at two."

"Fast figuring, Holmes . . ." George lifted his finger, so Pat corrected herself. "Sorry. Fast figuring, *Condo.*"

"Elementary, my dear Whatzit," George replied. "See you at two. Ta-ta."

* * *

The weather was deteriorating as George drove a beat-up station wagon north on the West Side Highway. A tweedily costumed "Dr. Whatzit" bounced uncomfortably by his side.

"I hope they have a good dentist at The Qualms," Pat said.

"A dentist? What for?" George asked.

"Because your car is loosening my fillings," Pat said.

"This isn't my car. Martha took the Jag. I rented this one," George explained.

"From who? Accidents-R-Us?" Pat asked.

"Whom," George corrected, "from whom, not 'from who.' And what's the matter with it?"

"I have seen better cars than this one turned into planters," Pat complained. She tried to roll down the window. The handle came off in her hand. "It's like riding in a dumpster. How much did they pay you to take this out of their sight for the weekend?"

"There's the George Washington Bridge," George said, coaxing the car toward the right-hand lanes. "Take a nap, Pard. I'll wake you in a while."

"I'll try, but I've never had much luck sleeping inside cement mixers." In two minutes Pat was asleep.

George drove for two hours, and the further north he drove the worse the weather became. "Certainly is nice weather for a murder," George mused. He reached out his window and whacked a windshield wiper blade that didn't want to wipe windshields any more. It cleared the window just in time for George to see a sign. He shook Pat gently by the shoulder.

"I don't want to go to school today, Mom," Pat said drowsily.

"Our exit is coming up, Dr. Whatzit," George intoned in the voice of Condo, "so perhaps you would care to navigate for us."

"Righto," harrumphed Whatzit. She sat up and scanned the map. "We take Route 28 to Route 42."

"Here's Route 28," George said, urging his rattletrap onto the off-ramp.

"Looks like we could be in for a bit of a blow, Condo," Pat said in stiff British tones.

"Pray conceal your weather observations, Whatzit,

lest they become reality," George cautioned.

The car dribbled along a two-lane road for many miles. "There should be a sign around here for The Qualms, according to this brochure," Pat said after an hour or so.

George slowed the car. "There." Pat pointed. "What's that just across the bridge?"

They stared past the car's hood at a wooden suspension bridge that had seen better days. Beyond it was a fork in the road and a weathered sign. An arrow mounted above the sign pointed to the left.

"That's it," George said. "The Qualms to the left. Excellent observation, my dear Whatzit."

But Pat had already shifted her attention to the bridge. "George, do you think that bridge will hold this car?" she asked in a worried voice.

"Of course. They put on these mystery weekends all the time. They just fix it up so it looks scary and unsafe," George reassured her. "Lighten up, Whatzit. And remember, it's Sherlock, not George. We have to stay in character," he scolded as he slowly nudged the raggedy car across the rickety bridge. Pat poked her head out the window for a better look, just as lightning lit up a deep ravine below them. Pat swallowed hard.

The car crawled across the swaying, moaning bridge. Pat didn't breathe again until they reached the muddy, rutted road on the other side of the gorge.

"Look," George said. "It's just like one of those old horror movies."

Pat looked. Lightning flashed again, and she saw a huge, gargoyle-encrusted manor house. "You'd be a terrific real estate agent, Sherlock," Pat said, shuddering.

George drove the car up to the house and parked under a portico. He forced his stoved-in door open, grabbed the luggage, and ran with Pat to the entrance of The Qualms. The door, at least ten feet high, was a formidable oak slab with a large iron knocker. George lifted the knocker and let it fall heavily against the base plate. The sound echoed through the night.

Presently the giant door creaked open. George and Pat took a nervous step back, not certain what would greet them. It turned out to be nothing more sinister than a tall man in butler's attire. He held up a candelabra and peered at the Mathnetters curiously. "Yes?"

George said, "I'm Sherlock Condo and this is my partner, Doctor . . ."

"Whatzit," Pat continued, to which both added, "Mathnet."

"Mathnet?" the butler asked, sounding angry.

"Sorry," George apologized. "Force of habit. We won't go out of character again. Who are you?"

"I am Peeved," the butler announced, looking down his large nose.

"I'm a little ticked off myself," George said. Peeved looked pained. It wasn't the first time he'd heard that one. "Have the other guests arrived?" George added.

"Why, yes," Peeved said, turning to indicate the interior of the mansion. "They're in the drawing room."

"Come along, Whatzit," George said, handing Peeved the suitcases and pushing past the servant. "We shall join the other players."

Pat and George marched along a hallway and into a large paneled drawing room. Paintings of frowning ancestors covered the walls, lighted by sconces. Suits of knights' armor stood as silent sentries about the room, and French doors appeared to open onto a veranda. Six guests were strewn about in high-backed wing chairs.

George cleared his throat. "I apologize for the lateness of the hour, but the weather was our enemy. I am Sherlock Condo and this is my colleague, Dr. Whatzit."

An elderly gentleman in a U.S. Army uniform snapped to attention, clicking his heels. In a very polished and clipped British accent he said, "I say, Condo, have you some perception as to what in the name of heaven is going on here?"

"I do indeed," George said. He removed an envelope from his tweed jacket, but before opening it, studied the man in front of him. "Who might you be?"

"I, sir, am Colonel Ashby Wiggins, U.S. Army, retired."

"If you were with the U.S. Army, why do you have a British accent?" Pat asked, whipping out her notebook.

"I was captured," the Colonel said briefly. He looked away, his stiff upper lip trembling.

George nodded in sympathy and opened his envelope. "I think we may as well begin," he said. "As captain of this event, I must inform you that one of us is responsible for the disappearance of our host, Mr. Barton Big. We all have motives, but only one of us is guilty. Our job is to find the criminal."

"What are you talking about?" demanded a tall and attractive young woman.

"Who are you, ma'am?" Pat asked, her pencil poised to record the answer.

"I'm Kitty Feline, a world-renowned dentist and recipient of the Nobel Teeth Prize," Kitty said, revealing a toothy smile. "I won it for flossing." Her smile vanished. "But I don't know any Mr. Big."

"What about the rest of you?" George asked.

"I'm Amanda Plonk, and I don't know what you're talking about either," said another woman. She didn't look up from her game of three-dimensional tic-tac-toe.

"What do you do in real life?" George asked her.

"I'm a professional quiz show contestant," she said, not without pride.

"A quiz show contestant?" Pat asked skeptically.

"It satisfies my inner greed," Ms. Plonk said, shrugging. The other three guests introduced themselves as Miles Reed, Wally Wallaby and Sally Storm. George was about to question them when Peeved interrupted.

"May it please the assemblage, dinner will be served shortly. Perhaps you'd care to dress."

"Right," George said. "Where shall I freshen up?"

Peeved raised his nose and sniffed. "Everywhere," he suggested. "Walk this way."

The butler led the group of eight up a wide, winding staircase. At the top was an easel supporting a diagram of the floor plan for the upstairs level. They gathered about the diagram.

"You will note that each of you has been assigned a bedroom. Each room is named for a color," Peeved pointed out. "You are expected in the dining room in fifteen minutes, at five minutes to eight."

Peeved left the group to puzzle out their rooms.

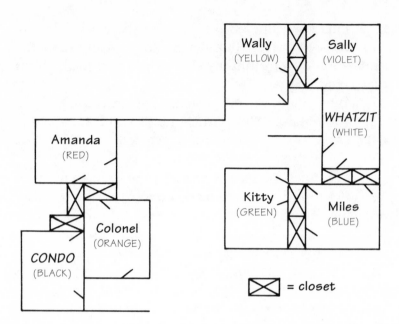

"You're in the White Room, Pat," George said, checking the chart. Their two names looked as if they had been added hurriedly. "I'm back here in the Black Room."

"See you downstairs for din-din," Pat said, then went to her room.

* * *

Precisely fifteen minutes later, the guests gathered for dinner and were seated at an elegantly appointed table. Pat leaned across a corner of the polished wood and whispered to George. "Pretty spiffy, huh, Pard?"

"I'll say," George agreed. "It's the spiffiest."

"How are your digs?"

"The room is fine but there's hardly any closet space. I practically had to wad my clothes up to fit them all in. How about yours?"

"Fine. Plenty of closet space," Pat said smugly.

As the other guests finished slurping their consommé, George watched Peeved carving something on a silver serving tray. "What's for eats, Peeved?"

Pat kicked George under the table.

"I mean," George corrected himself, "what are you carving for our repast, my man?"

"Wild boar," Peeved replied.

"Wild boar? Never had it," George said.

"I am amazed," Peeved mumbled, looking not in the least amazed.

Pat looked up as a grandfather clock began to chime the hour. She pointed to an empty chair and said, "We're missing someone. Perhaps we should wait."

Before anyone could reply, there was a crash of thunder, and a terrifying scream rang throughout the house. The diners looked wide-eyed, one to the other. "What was that?" Colonel Wiggins barked.

Miles Reed cocked his head. "B-flat, man."

A second scream, even more frightening than the first, bellowed forth.

"It's coming from upstairs," George said. The others bolted from the table and rushed up the stairs. George restrained Pat with a hand on her arm. Pat was surprised to see him smiling gleefully. "Is this a great game, or what?"

DUM DE DUM DUM

CHAPTER
2

Pat rushed up the stairs as George, pipe in hand, strolled casually after her. They found the others milling about in the upstairs landing near the room chart.

"Which of us is missing?" George asked.

"I believe it was the quiz show contestant," said Kitty, looking over the group.

Pat consulted her notebook. "Amanda Plonk," she announced as George reviewed the floor plan.

"She was in the Red Room," he said, pointing to the chart. George led the way. Outside the door of the Red Room, George put a cautionary finger to his lips. Then he thrust open the door, rushing in. He found a room filled with decorative scarlet touches—a red rug, roses, and wallpaper—but no Amanda. The room was empty.

"She's gone," said Colonel Wiggins in a grim voice.

George, peering through his magnifying glass, was scanning the room for clues. "What are you doing, Condo?" the Colonel asked.

"Looking for . . . hello? What's this?" George said, plucking a newspaper clipping from the top of a dresser.

Pat took and clipping and read, "'Amanda Wine Found Not Guilty.'"

"I thought it was Amanda Plonk," George said.

Pat read on. "'At eight o'clock last night, Amanda Wine walked through the halls of justice, a free woman. She was found not guilty of her accused crime of slandering President Grover Cleveland.'"

"But where is she . . . this Amanda Plonk or Amanda Wine or whomever?" the Colonel wanted to know.

"Not whomever, *whoever*." Even in the midst of mystery, George couldn't resist giving a grammar lesson.

"Whatever," retorted the Colonel, dismissively waving his hand. "The point is, she's gone."

Pat said, "Someone wrote a note on this clipping."

"What does it say?" asked Kitty Feline.

"It doesn't 'say' anything, Ms. Feline," George said, happy to continue his lesson. "You have to *read* it."

The guests looked like they were going to teach George a lesson, so Pat hurriedly read the note. "Someone wrote 'Justice will be done' in red ink. "

"Sounds rather ominous," George said happily. "Hello, what's this?" He bent down and picked up a small statue of a blindfolded and robed woman holding a scale. "A statuette representing blind justice." He put the clue in his pocket. "I suggest we repair to the dining room, finish our dinners and ask a few questions."

The others filed downstairs. George whispered to Pat, "I didn't know the *guests* were supposed to disappear. Kind of a neat wrinkle, don't you think?"

"If you say so, George," Pat said in a puzzled voice.

Back at the table, George took control of the questioning again. "Now then, let's find out why you people wanted to get rid of our host, Barton Big."

Colonel Wiggins held up his hand and said, "I don't mean to seem perverse, Condo, but don't you think we should call the local constabulary?"

"The police? Why?" George asked in amazement.

"Because one of our guests is missing, you clod, and the cops might just help find her," the Colonel snapped, losing his cool and his accent.

"Yes," said Wally Wallaby, a quiet, shy, round little man. "I think so, too."

Pat frowned. She thought she recognized Wally's whispering voice. "You look familiar," she told him.

"I used to do a children's TV show called 'Wally Wallaby and the Gang,'" Wally answered.

"I remember that show, man," said Miles.

"Oh, you do?" said Wally Wallaby, bouncing up and down on his chair.

"Yeah," Miles went on, "it was terrible."

"But to return to the plot," George said, "why did you want to do away with our host, Barton Big?"

"Willikers, I didn't. I wouldn't want to harm anyone ever in any way," Wally said with the sincerity of a TV personality. "I don't know anyone named Big."

George nodded. "All right, if that's your story. What about you, Mr. Reed?"

"Hey, man, Miles Reed just 'blows,' he don't 'off.' I ain't hip to a cat named 'Big.' I mean, he sounds like a 'suit,' man, and I don't hang with 'suits.'"

George looked at Pat helplessly. She interpreted.

"He said he just plays jazz sax, he doesn't kill people. And he says Mr. Big sounds like a business executive and he, Miles, does not make friends with business executives, nor does he know anyone with the last name of Big." Pat smiled at Miles's surprised look.

"I see," said George. He turned to Sally Storm. "We seem to have heard from everyone but you."

"I am an actress. You may have seen me on the day-time drama titled 'All My Doctors'?" She looked around smugly. Everyone looked at her blankly.

"Actresses always have something to hide in these mystery games," George mused. "Why did you want Mr. Big out of the way, Ms. Storm? Was he threatening you with something from your lurid past?"

"I have never heard of the man," said the flamboyant luminary. She folded her napkin and stood. "Now if you will excuse me, I am going to retire," she announced grandly, tossing her long hair as she flounced off.

"Yes," George agreed, "perhaps we should all turn in for the evening and begin afresh anon."

"Afresh anon?" said Miles, scratching his goatee. "What do you a-mean, a-man?"

Pat did a reverse interpretation for the jazzman. "He says we should all sack out and hit the groove again in the morning." Miles smiled at her gratefully.

Wally was still nervous. "I think we should call the police."

"And ruin the game?" George admonished.

"I don't know about any game, but I think a good night's rest might help us all. Good night, troops," said

Colonel Wiggins. He saluted and left the room.

The others followed suit and went upstairs to their rooms, bidding one another pleasant dreams.

* * *

Flossing in his bathroom, George paused as he heard the strains of a beautiful alto saxophone solo wafting through the house. "Must be Miles Reed," George said to himself. He smiled and climbed into bed.

George had just drifted off to sleep when he was jolted awake by what sounded like a man's scream. He bolted from bed, threw on his velvet dressing gown and burst through the door into the hall. It was empty. George shrugged and closed the door.

"Must have been the storm," George said, plumping his pillow and snuggling back into bed. "Boy, what a mystery weekend. It's got everything."

The other guests tentatively poked their sleepy heads from their doors. Noting one another and smiling sheepishly, they returned to their beds.

Moments later, George heard another scream. He put on his robe and opened the door to find Pat and the others looking very, very worried.

"George," Pat said, "are you all right?"

"Of course," George said, moving into the hall.

"Then Colonel Wiggins isn't," Pat said, counting heads. "He's the only one not accounted for."

"Really?" said George. Shaking off sleep, he slid back into his Condo character and pulled his curved pipe from his dressing gown pocket.

Miles Reed stared at the pipe. "Wow, man, I never saw a sax in the toddler stage before."

"George," Pat said with concern, "I don't think this game is on the up and up."

"Don't be silly, Whatzit," George soothed. "Now then, did we all hear some screams?"

"Of course we heard screams, you nit. Why do you think we're out here in the middle of the night in our jammies?" Sally Storm raged.

"Wiggins was in the Orange Room," Pat said. "It's the one next to yours, Sherlock."

George led the way into the Orange Room, which was indeed orange. It was also empty. Pat picked up another news clipping.

"'Wiggston Is Freed,'" she read.

"I thought his name was Wiggins." George frowned, moving about the room and poking into the closet. "How come everyone gets a bigger closet than I do?" he whined. "Amanda's was bigger than mine, too."

Pat shrugged and continued reading. "'At exactly 10:13 Col. Ashby Wiggston left Federal Court a free man after having been found not guilty of the charge of stealing rare coins.'"

Pat turned the clipping around. "Same note . . . 'Justice will be done.'"

Miles retrieved a second statuette of blind justice from the floor. "Same chick, man." Miles handed the statuette to George as the group moved into the hall.

Pat grabbed the floor plan off its easel and tried to re-create the scene. "Now," she said to the assembled group, "what happened after we heard the first scream?"

"I opened my door and peeked out," said Kitty.

"That's right, man," attested Miles. "I saw you."

Pat said, "And I opened my door . . ."

"I saw you, too, man," Miles said.

"And I saw you and Kitty," Pat agreed. "Those lines of sight check out on the floor plan."

"I opened my door and saw no one," George said. He pointed to his room on the chart. "I thought the first scream was just the wind and went back inside."

"When I opened my door I saw Sally Storm," said Wally Wallaby. He stared soulfully at the glamorous actress. Sally looked grateful for the attention.

"And I saw you, Wally," she said, looking deeply into Wally's eyes.

"Well," George summarized, "everyone here was seen so none of us could have been prowling around the corridor sneaking into the colonel's room."

"Everyone but you, Sherlock," Sally said.

"Yeah, man," Miles added, "nobody saw *you*."

"But . . . but . . ." George spluttered.

"That's ridiculous." Pat leapt to the defense of her partner. "He's the captain of this mystery weekend."

"Mystery weekend?" Wally looked confused.

"*Most* of my weekends are mysteries to me, man," Miles put in.

Sally Storm said, "I don't know what any of you is talking about so I'm going back to bed."

Pat concurred. "Let's all get back to bed. And lock your doors," she warned.

As the rest of the group shuffled back toward their rooms, Pat grabbed George's arm. "George, I think we've got more than a mystery weekend on our hands. I think we've got a real mystery."

George looked stunned. "You think this might be real life?"

"Yes," she said, "and I think we should call the cops."

George protested as Pat hustled him down the stairs. "Pat, I feel silly calling the police just because a few people on a mystery weekend have disappeared."

Pat moved toward the phone in the hallway. "People on mystery weekends aren't supposed to disappear, George. Something in this equation just doesn't figure."

Reluctantly, George disengaged the receiver and dialed "0." "Hello, Operator, I'd like the police . . . hello? Hello?" He turned to Pat and smiled. "Well, I don't need to feel silly about phoning the police."

"Why not?"

George's smile faded. "Because the phone is dead."

DUM DE DUM DUM

CHAPTER
3

The storm was still raging a few minutes later as George, clad in a yellow slicker, made his way outside.

"This is not ideal weather for a stroll," George said to himself. He directed his flashlight beam against the side of the house. "Those phone wires have got to be here somewhere," he said, squinting into the driving rain.

George turned his back to the wind and stepped backwards along the side of the house, inspecting as he went. He came to a corner, and as he stepped beyond the protective confines of the wall, he lurched heavily against something . . . or someone. He spun quickly, raising the flashlight above his head. He was about to bring it down on his assailant when . . .

"George, don't!" Pat shouted through the wind.

"Pat, what are you doing out here?" George yelled.

"I thought two sets of eyes might be 'wetter' than one." Pat turned and waved at George to follow. "I want to show you something."

The twosome slogged through the muddy terrain as lightning exploded and thunder crashed around them. Pat led George toward the road. She stopped beside a pole and pointed her light upward. "Look."

A loose wire dangled from the pole. George avoided the swaying line but caught a glimpse of its neatly clipped end.

"It looks like it was deliberately cut. But why?"

"Someone doesn't want any phone calls coming in or going out," Pat surmised. She exchanged grim looks with her partner. "Still think it's a game, Sherlock?"

"I'm afraid not," George answered. He struck off toward his car. "Come on, we're going for the police."

They arrived at the front of the house, only to find that the car was not under the portico where George had left it. "This is crazy," George said, looking around. "Who would want an old junker like that?"

"Maybe someone doesn't want us to leave here, either," Pat said.

George thought a moment, then pointed to the house. "You stay here until I get back."

"Back from where?"

"I'm going to get the police."

"On foot?" Pat looked anxiously at her partner's feet. They wore stylish but soggy oxfords.

Pat argued with George about him going off alone until he persuaded her that someone had to stay behind to warn the other guests, just in case anything happened to him. "Just don't *let* anything happen," Pat yelled as she watched him head off toward the town of Bile.

George had trouble even finding the rutted road they

had driven on. It was more a river than a road. He pressed on, slipping and sliding down a treacherous grade as his flashlight began to go dim, dimmer and dimmest, finally leaving George in darkness, standing knee-deep in mud. He slipped and fell with every second step. He cursed himself for getting involved in this crazy mystery weekend.

George struggled along the road, muttering to himself. "The bridge should be around here somewhere."

Suddenly George fell again. But this time he began to slide. He tried to brake himself, but his body was picking up speed. He was going down and he was going down fast.

"The road wasn't *this* steep," George gasped, his mind reeling. Then he remembered. "The ravine!"

George grasped wildly for something to stop his slide. He clutched at a small tree, but his weight and speed pulled it out of the wet soil like a dandelion.

Then George's hand grasped something solid. He hooked his arm about it. His terrifying slide stopped.

In a flash of lightning George saw that his body was wrapped around one of the posts which had held the rickety suspension bridge. A second flash revealed the bridge—it had collapsed into the ravine.

George let out his breath as he realized how close he had come to death. His legs were so weak he needed to crawl up to the road and grab The Qualms' signpost to get to his feet. That's when George noticed something about the sign. The arrow was pointing right instead of left. As he blinked through the rain, George got another glimpse, and this time the arrow was simply spinning in the wind, broken. "No wonder those nuts think we're nuts." George shook his head. "We're not at The Qualms after all."

George began trudging slowly back toward the house. There was no question now—they had a real mystery on their hands. And a real criminal.

* * *

Meanwhile, back at the mansion, Pat sat at the game table in the drawing room pondering the game of 3-D tic-tac-toe. In addition to playing the game of X's and O's vertically, horizontally and diagonally, this game added the feature of depth and made it much more challenging. "But it's not as challenging as our mystery," Pat said quietly to herself, giving her watch a worried glance.

Pat got up and began to pace the room. "I wonder," she muttered, "how long it will take George to walk to town." Pat was trying to set up a mental estimation equation when she heard a sound. It was coming from the French doors leading to the veranda. Pat spun to face the doors. They were being forced open. Pat grabbed a heavy candlestick and rushed to the flimsy doors. She threw her body against them but was a second too late. She was pushed aside as a body hurtled into the room. Pat lifted the candlestick over her head. She was about to bring it down on the intruder when . . . "Pat are you okay?" The muddy body rolled over, and George Frankly ripped off his waterproof hat.

"George! What happened to you?" Pat gasped. She dropped the candlestick and helped George to his feet.

"Before or after I almost fell into the ravine?" George asked. He stripped off his muddy slicker and tossed it aside. "I'm okay. What about you?"

"I'm fine. Did you get to the police?"

"No, I didn't. And they can't get to us because the bridge is out. We are cut off for now," George announced. "We'd better wake the others and tell them."

"Tell them what?" inquired a voice behind them.

Pat and George jumped. They turned quickly to see that Peeved had entered the room.

"Oh, it's you, Peeved," Pat acknowledged, sighing in relief. "We didn't hear you come in."

"I didn't mean to startle," the butler apologized.

"Peeved," George said, "we signed up for this mystery weekend at a manor house called The Qualms . . ."

"I know nothing about mystery weekends, but this is very definitely *not* The Qualms," Peeved said. He wiped a speck of dust from a tabletop with one gloved hand. "You're at Wit's End."

George and Pat looked at each other resignedly.

"I fear you made a wrong turn. The Qualms is one mountain top over . . . to the right," Peeved said.

"Well, then, who are these people?" Pat asked.

Peeved looked at them blankly. "I don't know."

George was determined to get some answers from the man. "Peeved, who owns this place?"

"I'm sure I don't know that either, sir," Peeved responded. "I have been the sole servant at Wit's End for fifteen years and I have never met the owner."

"Is he or she ever here?" Pat asked.

"Yes," Peeved replied. "The owner is very reclusive. I am simply left money and lists of things to take care of. I take meals to the master bedroom, leave them outside and pick up the dishes later."

"What were your instructions for this weekend?" Pat continued.

"They were to prepare the house for six people. The owner will arrive on the morrow." Peeved winced as a crack of thunder rocked the house. "However, with this storm, there may be a delay."

"So you prepared for six guests and then we showed up, too," George said.

"Yes, which is why I appeared a bit surprised when you arrived, making guests seven and eight." Peeved forced a smile. "But no matter. I am certain you are most welcome by the master." The butler turned to go.

"Is there a basement in this house?" Pat asked.

"No," Peeved said, "the house is built on a rock ledge."

"Any secret rooms where the kidnapped guests might be kept?" Pat continued.

Peeved shook his head. "I fear not."

George reached into his pocket and removed the statuette of blind justice he had removed from Wiggins's room. "Know anything about this?"

Peeved shook his head. "No," he said, "except that there have always been several of them on the bookcase." He pointed with his thumb toward the far wall. There were three statuettes standing in a row on the top shelf.

"Several?" Pat asked.

"Six to be precise," Peeved answered. When Pat posed no more questions he left the room.

Pat and George looked at the statuettes. "And then there were three," Pat said with a dramatic flair.

George sat down. "That makes no sense. Three statuettes are gone and only *two* guests are missing."

"I guess that means kidnapping number three is already being planned," Pat pondered. "But who could be committing the crimes?"

George had brought the floor plan downstairs earlier that day. "I'll tell you who *couldn't* have done it."

Pat watched as George pointed to the chart.

"Look," George said. "When we heard Colonel Wiggins scream, you were in the White Room and said you saw Kitty in the Green Room and Miles in the Blue Room."

Pat nodded in agreement. "So they're not guilty of prowling the halls," she said.

"And Wally said he saw Sally in the Violet Room and Sally saw Wally in the Yellow Room, so that lets them out," George concluded.

"But, George," Pat said, "no one *else* saw Sally and Wally. What if they're in it together?"

"Sure," George said, "the two of them could have grabbed Colonel Wiggins and . . ."

George's final summation was interrupted by another scream. It sounded like a man and it came from upstairs. Pat and George raced up the staircase. Frightened faces popped out as doors opened. George scanned them quickly and said, "Wally Wallaby."

"The Yellow Room," Pat said, pointing.

George burst in, turned on the lights, and found an empty, golden room. "Kind of punches holes in the Sally-Wally conspiracy theory," George sighed as Pat picked up a statuette and a press clipping.

"'Waffle Walks. Wallace Waffle was found innocent of bank robbery and walked away a free man at 11:05 today.'" Pat turned the paper so they could see the blurred letters spelling "Justice will be done."

"Poor Wally," Sally Storm sniffled.

"At least he had a bigger closet than I have," George tried to console her.

"Stop whining, Pard," Pat chided. She began herding the shrinking party out the door. "I think it's time we searched the house for our friends."

* * *

They searched the house from top to bottom and found no sign of the missing guests.

George explained who he and Pat were, then began some serious questioning. "How did you people get here?"

"We all rode up from Manhattan in a mini-van," answered Kitty Feline.

"And none of you had met before?" Pat asked.

"That's right," answered Sally Storm.

George paced the room and took three printed invitations from his pocket. "These are invitations our three missing guests received. Each says, 'Come to Wit's End next Friday and watch justice be done.'" He looked at the others. "Did you receive the same letters?"

The three nodded.

"But," Pat offered, "these invitations were addressed to Colonel Ashby Wiggston, Amanda Wine and Wallace Waffle—not the names our friends were using here."

"So?" queried Kitty, her eyebrows arching.

"So . . . we'd like to see your invitations," Pat continued. "Miles Reed?"

"Yeah, man," Miles said reluctantly. He reached in his pocket for his invitation and surrendered it to Pat.

"Miles Toogo?" Pat said, lifting an eyebrow.

"So I changed my name from Miles Toogo to Miles Reed. That ain't no crime, man," Miles said angrily.

"And you?" Pat said to Sally Storm. "Did you change your name as well?"

"Yes, from Sally Stoop to Sally Storm," the actress admitted.

"Kitty Kat to Kitty Feline," the dentist allowed.

George nodded, his suspicions confirmed. "Perhaps it's time to play What Do We Know?" he suggested.

"It's a way of organizing facts and attempting to solve a problem," Pat explained to the puzzled guests.

"We know that the three guests who disappeared were accused of crimes," George began.

"We know each was found not guilty," added Pat.

"We know that all had changed their names," George continued.

"And that they all received invitations to this event addressed to them using their old names," Pat went on.

"And we know," Sally said, "that we don't know why they were kidnapped."

"Hey, man, we don't even dig why any of those cats were at this gig," Miles said. He seated himself at the piano and noodled a riff on the keyboard.

"What did he say?" George asked Pat.

"He said we don't know why any of them were here," Pat decoded.

"Yes," George said, "why *did* you people come here? If I had gotten an unsigned invitation I would have figured it was junk mail. But you all took it seriously."

"Because the invitation was addressed to a name I haven't used in years," Sally said.

"That's right," agreed Kitty.

"Hey, man, they nailed it. I mean if someone is going through my dirty laundry, I want to know who and why," Miles concluded.

George frowned at Miles a moment, then shrugged.

"Let me hypothesize," he began.

"In front of the ladies?" Miles asked.

"Let me try a theory," George tried again. He pointed his pipe at the guests. "Was each of you accused of a crime in your past?"

Miles, Sally and Kitty looked at one another, then down at the floor. Each slowly nodded yes.

"And was each of you found innocent?"

Again they nodded, more eagerly this time.

"And were you tried under your real names?"

Yes was the answer.

"And were your cases all played up in the press and on radio and television?"

"Hey, man," Miles said, "my case was the reason they invented expanded local coverage."

Pat waded into the discussion. "Your cases made you all somewhat notorious, even though you were judged not guilty, so you changed your names, right?"

Sally leaned back in her chair and sighed. "Even though I was innocent, I felt my career would be clouded and I would have trouble getting acting roles."

"I felt that way, too," Kitty said. " People need to trust their health care professionals."

"That's it, man," Miles agreed. "Sad but true. I even had to go from tenor sax to alto just to hide."

"A pattern is starting to emerge," Pat said to George.

"Yes," he said. "Maybe we can find other things you might have in common. When you were on trial, did you have the same judge?"

"Mine," Sally said, "was a judge named Larry."

"Curly," said Miles.

"Moe," Kitty added.

"Okay," Pat said, "you had different judges. How about defense attorneys?"

Again the threesome chimed.

"Tinker."

"Evers."

"Chance."

George shook his head. "How about the prosecutor? Was that the same person?"

Miles said, "Mine was a D.A. named Patty."

"Maxine."

"And Laverne," finished Kitty.

Pat scratched her head and said, "There has to be another pattern."

Sally rose from her chair. "I think I'll ask Peeved to brew us some tea," she said, and left the room.

George was examining the news clippings. "Hey, Pat. Here's a pattern. The first guest to be snatched was . . ."

"Amanda Wine," Pat said.

"Right," the mathematician said. "Her trial was in March. Colonel Wiggston was next and his trial was in April. Wally was third and his trial was in May. Maybe they're being kidnapped in that order."

"Miles," Pat mused. "When were you exonerated?"

Miles thought. "It was when they make all those loud explosions, man."

"Fourth of July?" George asked.

"Right on," Miles said, returning to the piano.

"I was tried in June," Kitty said.

"If Sally Storm was found not guilty in August we may be on to something," George said. "Of course, it doesn't tell us who or why, just when."

Pat picked up the pile of invitations. "The postmarks on these are all from Bile," she noted.

"You mean they were all mailed nearby?" George said. "Maybe Peeved mailed them."

"Maybe Peeved wrote them," Pat added. "But that would mean the butler did it." Everyone groaned.

Just then another scream pierced the night. Sally Storm rushed into the room, her eyes wide. "Come quickly . . . it's Peeved. I think he may be . . . he may be . . ."

George rushed past the actress, who was looking for an appropriate chair to faint onto. The group burst into the kitchen to find Peeved's crumpled body on the floor. A heavy skillet lay on the floor nearby. George knelt beside Peeved and felt for a pulse.

"George," Pat said fearfully, "is he . . ."

"I'll say he is," George said solemnly. "He's been knocked out cold."

DUM DE DUM DUM

CHAPTER
4

"I wonder how much rain has fallen during this storm," Kitty mused, looking out the window.

"All of it, man," said Miles, paging through a coffee table book of Modern Art. "This stuff is wild," Miles said, scrutinizing a Cubist painting.

Sally glanced at it, then said to Miles, "You've got the book upside down."

Pat looked up as George entered the room.

"He'll be okay," George announced. "He's groggy and has a knot on his beezer the size of a goose egg."

"Where is he?" Pat asked.

"I gave him a sedative and put him to bed. He'll sleep like a baby until morning and then wake up with a terrible headache," George said.

"I wonder who conked the old sideman," Miles said, turning his art book right side up. He took one look and turned it upside down again.

"Well," Pat said, "it couldn't have been one of us. . . . We were all together."

"Not really," Kitty Kat said. "Ms. Sally Stoop was in the kitchen with Peeved."

Sally rose from her chair majestically. "How dare you!" she gasped. "I don't have to sit here and stand for this. I'm going to lie down."

"Wait," said George sternly. "I think we should all stay together here until morning. It will be safer."

"When I wonder what you think, I'll ask you," Sally snapped. "Good night. Or what's left of it."

Kitty Kat also arose. "I don't trust her being away from the group. If she goes, I go."

"Me, too, man," said Miles, taking a long hard look at the room chart. "I'm outta here."

The Mathnetters tried to persuade the others to stay, but they were too tired and upset to listen to reason.

Pat and George watched the survivors climb the stairs and heard their doors slam shut. George looked thoughtful as he wandered into the billiard room.

Pat sat on a chair and looked pensive. "George," she said, "I asked Sally about her trial. It was in December. The timing theory is shot."

"Rats," said George, lining up seven pool balls in a v-shape on the felt-topped pool table.

"But you know," Pat went on, "Sally *was* alone with Peeved. She could be the culprit."

"I thought of that," George said. He carefully placed the cue ball on the table. "Peeved is tall and was hit on the top of the head. Unless Sally was standing on a chair or something, she's too short to have hit him. Even so, I'm not sure she is strong enough to knock him out."

Pat watched George idly. Just as he was about to

shoot, she asked, "What kind of pool game is that? Why aren't you using all fifteen balls?"

"There are lots of pool games, Pat," George said patiently. "This one uses seven balls and is called Color Pool because it uses the colors on the color wheel. See?" He pointed to the balls with his cue stick. "Red, orange, yellow, green, blue, and violet," he said. He pointed again with the cue. "Plus black and white."

Suddenly Pat shot to her feet and ran out of the room. In a moment she was back, carrying the floor plan. "Look at the rooms," she spluttered. "Each is a color on the wheel, and look at the order of disappearance. First was Amanda in the Red Room . . . then the Colonel in the Orange Room and finally, Wally in the Yellow Room. They go in order of the color spectrum. It might be a pattern."

In his excitement George shot the cue ball without looking. He hit the massed balls squarely, sending them hurtling across the table and into the pockets. He scored six of the seven balls.

"You shoot a good game with that stick," said Pat.

"I had a misspent youth," George replied. "If you're right about the pattern," he said, picking the green six ball out of the corner pocket, "green's next."

Pat looked at the chart and pointed to the Green Room. "That's Kitty Kat."

"Yes, Pard," George said, "but the guests are locked in their rooms and Peeved is out cold, so unless one of *us* does it, there's no one left to do the kidnapping."

Pat had to agree. George leaned his elbow on the mantelpiece of the fireplace. He looked at the news clippings again. In a moment he straightened, almost stepping into the blazing logs in his excitement.

"When you read these clippings, did you notice anything unusual about them?" George asked Pat.

"Not particularly," she answered. "Why? Have you found something?"

"In every lead the reporter mentions the time the defendant was released," George said. "It's a rather clumsy writing style and time is not important to the story. Who cares that Amanda Wine was released at exactly eight o'clock or Colonel Wiggston was freed at 10:03?"

Pat snapped her fingers. "George," she said, "Amanda was kidnapped at exactly eight o'clock. I know because I remember the grandfather clock was chiming. What time was the Colonel grabbed?"

"I don't know," George said. He frowned in thought. "Around ten, I think."

"Wally was kidnapped a little after eleven because the clock had chimed just before we heard him scream. What does the news article say about time?"

George consulted the Waffle clipping. "11:05," he said. "You know, Pat . . . if the same reporter wrote all these stories, maybe he's our kidnapper."

"Isn't there a byline on the stories?" Pat asked. "You know, the thing that identifies the reporter?"

"No," George said, scanning the papers, "just signature initials at the bottom of the column . . . J.F."

"J.F.," Pat repeated. "There was a famous reporter with *The New York Past* named Jimmy Factless."

"Sure," George said, "I've heard of him. He's the guy who never lets truth get in the way of a good story. Maybe Jimmy Factless is our guy."

"We can call the paper tomorrow," Pat said.

"Yeah," George said, "if it isn't too late."

Pat stared at the shelf on the wall that held the statuettes of blind justice. Only two were left.

Pat was about to mention this to George when a woman's scream interrupted her. She looked at her watch and noted the time at 12:07.

"That's got to be Sally or Kitty," George said, leading the charge to the staircase.

"Kitty's in the Green Room," Pat shouted. "If the color theory holds, that's next."

The Mathnetters ran to the Green Room and George tried the door. It was locked. He pounded on it. "Kitty Kat . . . open up. It's George Frankly."

The door remained closed. George said, "You're going to have to break it down, Pat."

Pat stared at her partner in disbelief.

"I've got a bad shoulder," he explained feebly.

Suddenly the door opened inward. The duo stared at the person standing there.

"Miles Toogo . . ."

"Right on, man," said Miles.

"What are you doing in Kitty Kat's room? You're supposed to be in the Blue Room," George pointed out.

"I had a hunch, man, so we switched rooms," the reedman answered.

George rushed to the Blue Room and opened the door. The Blue Room was empty, save for a news clipping, a statuette and . . . "*Two* closets!" George grumbled.

"'At exactly 12:07, Kitty Kat became a free woman, found not guilty of a fur robbery in midtown,'" Pat read.

There was a moment's flurry when the door opened, but it was only Sally Storm. George turned to Miles.

"What was your hunch?" George asked.

"I noticed the snatches were going from hot to cool, man," the jazz player said, looking pleased with himself.

"Hot to cool? Like . . . in jazz?" Pat asked.

"No, man, like in colors. You dig? Hot colors like red to orange to yellow, to cool ones like green, blue and violet. I figured whoever was behind this gig was going in order of the color spectrum."

"So," Pat said, "you figured green would be next."

"You're hip, man," Miles acknowledged. "So I took the Green Room and figured I'd catch this cat when he made his move on Kitty. Didn't work. Bummer, man."

"But your heuristics were good," Pat enthused.

"No one ever laid that on me before," Miles admitted.

Sally was tired of being left out of the spotlight. "I can't stand much more of this," she emoted. "We're just lolling about this horrible place waiting to be spirited away in the night."

"Let's go downstairs," George said, descending the stairs to the drawing room. "Miles," he said, "do you remember what time you were released from court?"

"Time?" said Miles, sitting down at the piano as usual. "No way, man. Time is an arbitrary invention of the suits. If it ain't 5/4, I got no use for it." George stared at Miles with an icy countenance until the jazzman lost his cool.

"I don't know, man," Miles said. "Sometime around one, I think."

"I know exactly what time I was freed," Sally said, swooping into a chair with a book from the library. "It was

12:45. But what has that to do with anything?"

"Maybe nothing, but we're still looking for patterns," George explained. "If we go by time, Sally is next. If we go by color, Miles is next." George brightened. "We do have an idea about who's behind this case, though."

Sally looked shocked, Miles amazed.

"Lay it on the line man," Miles begged.

"Ever heard of a loud-mouthed, rude, biased newspaper reporter named Jimmy Factless?" Pat asked.

Miles slammed his hands on the piano keys. "He's the lowest, man. People start religions against guys like him."

"He may have covered all the trials for his newspaper. That's where those clippings came from. We think he's the one after you," George said.

"Good guess except for one thing, man," Miles said. "The cat took a left about a year ago."

"He died?" Pat decoded.

"He was hit by a newspaper truck," Sally added.

"You got it," Miles said, stifling a laugh. "It was delivering the rival paper, *The Daily Snooze*."

While Miles and Sally traded I-Hate-Factless stories, George sidled over to Pat. "If Factless is dead, maybe our crook is one of these two guys," he whispered. "I'll watch Miles; you keep an eye on Sally." Pat nodded approval.

"I don't know about you cats, but I'm going to grab some z's," Miles yawned. Of course, then Pat yawned and so did George and Sally.

"I'm not sleepy yet. I'll read a bit longer," Sally said, opening her book.

Pat stretched and pretended to follow Miles and George toward the stairs as they bid one another good-

night. Suddenly, she ducked down behind a gigantic palm tree and hid among its fronds where she could keep a trained eye on Sally Storm, a.k.a. Sally Stoop.

* * *

At last the house was silent . . . deathly silent. George had watched Miles enter the Blue Room. Then George stationed himself in the Green Room with the door slightly ajar so he could see if Toogo did go.

Pat remained behind the palm as the clock tick-tocked time relentlessly forward, chiming at 15-minute intervals as it neared one a.m. Sally continued to read.

At precisely 12:45, Pat heard a man's scream coming from upstairs. Abandoning her palm, Pat moved swiftly and took the stairs in twos. Suddenly she was blind-sided by her partner, who was hurtling *down* the stairs in *threes*.

45

"Are you all right?" they said together.

"George," Pat said, struggling to her feet, "what are you doing here? I heard a man scream upstairs."

"What?" George said with incredulity. "I just heard a *woman* scream *down*stairs."

"But . . ." Realization washed over both of them. George raced back upstairs and Pat ran to the library. Sally Storm was gone. Pat picked up a statuette and a clipping and sank into a chair with a look of devastation on her face. She looked up at George as he walked into the room. He shook his head, and the two exchanged clippings.

George read, "'Actress Found Not Guilty in Accident. At 12:45 today, Sally Stoop walked from the halls of justice, a free woman . . .'"

Pat read, "'Jazzman Not Responsible for Vanishing Violin. At 12:45 today, Miles Toogo shuffled into daylight, a free man . . .'"

"'Justice will be done,'" they both finished.

George pointed to the blind justice shelf. It was empty.

Pat sighed and said, "And then there were none."

DUM DE DUM DUM

CHAPTER
5

Pat was on the upstairs landing. She couldn't locate her partner. They had parted in order to search the house again, but now Pat wasn't so sure that had been a good idea. She moved stealthily from room to room, quietly opening doors and peering inside. Then she straightened suddenly. "Why am I being so quiet?" she asked herself loudly. "There are only two of us left. Hey, George!" she yelled. "Where the heck are you?"

"In here," Pat heard George reply. "In my room."

Pat found her partner heel-and-toeing across the width of the Black Room.

"New dance step, Pard?" she asked.

"I'm measuring," George said, stopping at the wall, "and I'm right."

"About what?" Pat wanted to know.

"My room is larger than the Blue, Red, and Violet Rooms by about three feet," he said triumphantly.

"So what?" Pat asked.

"On the diagram, all the rooms are shown to be about

the same size," George pointed out. "They aren't, and neither are the closets. Mine is shown to be the same size as the others but it's actually about half as big."

"Are you still complaining about that?" Pat wailed.

But George had entered his closet and was fighting his way through the clothes he'd stuffed in the small space. "I think whoever made the chart was trying to hide something strange about these rooms," came George's muffled voice.

"What are you doing, George?" Pat demanded.

George stumbled over one of his shoes and grabbed a coat hook for balance. The hook twisted in his hand, and a panel at the back of the closet slid open.

"Pat!" George said. "I've found a secret panel."

George pushed on and found himself in the closet in the Red Room. He twisted another hook and discovered a passage to the closet in the Orange Room.

George returned to Pat, smiling broadly. "Well, we know how our kidnapper moves around without being seen in the hallway. Let's go downstairs and check the floor plan," he suggested.

In the drawing room, George pointed at the room chart. "See. I bet the Yellow and Violet Rooms are connected by their closets, too."

"What about the other three rooms?" Pat asked.

"They're connected, too," George said.

"Yes," Pat agreed, "but they're disconnected from the other five by the hallways. And even if that's how he moved around, what did he do with his victims, hide them in closets?" She shook her head.

"Maybe he waited for everyone to go back to bed and

then moved them down the stairs," George hypothesized. "Although that would be awfully risky."

Pat sighed. "I don't know what difference any of this makes, because all of the suspects have been kidnapped," she said glumly, staring at the empty shelf.

"Leaving us with just one conclusion," George said.

"Which is?" Pat rejoined.

"One of us did it." George snickered.

Pat had to smile. She moved to the French doors and looked out. "The rain seems to have stopped finally," she reported, turning to look at George. Her partner was as pale as a sheet. "George, what's wrong?"

"Look," George said, pointing to the blind justice bookcase. There were two statuettes on the shelf.

"Those weren't there a moment ago," Pat said. "Maybe it means there's more justice to be done."

"What it means," George said grimly, as he moved to the shelf, "is there is someone else in this house and we are at risk."

George tapped the wall, and they heard a hollow sound. "Probably a secret panel here, but I can't find a release for it. Maybe it's on the inside of the wall," he said, looking at Pat. She was studying the 3-D tic-tac-toe game.

"George," she said in a funny voice, "we've been assuming that the upstairs rooms are connected only on the upstairs level. But look at this game," she went on. "It's in three dimensions—length, width and *depth*."

"I know, Pat," George said, looking at her as if she were crazy. "But I don't want to play now."

"We've been looking for ways to connect the disconnected rooms and for ways to move up and down stairs undetected. What if the second floor"—Pat pointed to the 3-D structure—"is secretly connected to the first floor?"

"How?" George was still puzzled.

"I don't know . . . a staircase?" Pat suggested.

"Not enough room."

"A spiral staircase in a secret panel?" Pat grabbed the room chart. "You said your room was bigger than some of the others."

"Yes," George agreed, "about three feet bigger."

Pat drew lines down the sides of the Red, Blue and Violet Rooms. "That's roughly three feet," she said.

"That would be enough room for a secret passage *and* a spiral stair," George admitted. "Okay, maybe we know 'how' but we still don't know 'who.' The victims were all kidnapped in the same manner, with a news clipping and a statuette left behind."

"All the victims were kidnapped except one . . ." Pat pointed out. "Peeved."

"Peeved," George echoed. "He was hit on the head. But maybe Sally interrupted the kidnapper before he could drag Peeved away," he reasoned.

"The kidnapper would have been seen," Pat argued. "There's only one way out of the kitchen." Her shoulders slumped. "Unless there's *another* secret passage."

"It's probably not he," George said, "but perhaps it's time for Dr. Frankly to pay a visit to Patient Peeved, just in case. I'll be right back."

When George had gone, Pat realized it wasn't wise to split up, so she too headed off toward the butler's room.

She arrived at Peeved's door and opened it. "George?" She looked inside and saw an empty room. "George, this is no time to be cute. George?" The bed was rumpled, and both Peeved and George were gone. Pat backed cautiously out of the room and walked slowly toward the billiard room.

"Well," she said aloud, "perhaps it's time to play What Do I Know? I know I am in a sinister mansion. I know six people have been kidnapped. I know George is missing, too. Ergo, I know . . . I'd better be careful."

She heard soft steps on the stairs and turned in relief, scolding, "George, where were you? I was . . . you're not George." Pat paused.

Standing on the bottom step was the butler, a large knot on his head and a maniac's gleam in his eyes.

"No," he said in a husky voice, "I am Peeved."

"Well," Pat tried for lightness, "I'm a little ticked."

"Don't run that line again," Peeved snarled, moving deliberately after her. Pat began to back into the billiard room.

"Sure thing," Pat agreed nervously, backing into the pool table. "It seems the butler really did do it."

Peeved growled.

"So," Pat chattered, edging around the pool table as Peeved stalked her, "you're behind this little gala, eh, Peeved?"

"I am," the crazed butler cackled. "Every step . . . every ploy . . . it's my plan . . . mine, do you hear me, all mine!"

"You're coming through loud and clear, Peeved. Tell me, where are the others?" Pat asked sweetly, maneuvering around the edge of the table.

"Incarcerated." Peeved feinted to the left.

"In Carcerated?" Pat feinted to the right. "Carcerated

is a little town in New Mexico, isn't it? Mighty pretty country out there. I had a brother-in-law from—"

"Enough!" Peeved howled. "You are about to join the others, my little mathematician."

"'Mathematician,'" Pat cooed. "I'll bet you say that to all the girls."

Peeved lunged at her, and Pat slipped to the other side of the table, careful to keep it between them.

"You're into math, Peeved?" Pat asked conversationally.

"I hate math! I *hate* it. That's why the others are here, because of math," Peeved said lunging again.

"You hate math? Perhaps you'd like to talk about it," Pat encouraged. Anything to stall for time.

"The others are guilty of crimes, but they were let off because of . . . mathematics," Peeved spat.

"Gee," Pat said, "I find that difficult to believe . . ."

Again Peeved lunged and fell heavily across the corner of the table.

"Not *impossible*, mind you," Pat continued, "just difficult. Peeved, who owns this place?"

"I do," said Peeved through clenched teeth. "This place is mine. It is my beloved sanctuary. I have been at my Wit's End since I left the courts."

"That's the truth," Pat said, trying to get up courage to make a break for the door. "The courts, eh? What did you do there before you do whatever it is you do now?"

"Court stenographer!" Peeved hissed, nearly catching hold of her arm.

"The person who takes down testimony in court cases?" Pat stopped dead in her tracks with surprise.

"The very same," the phony servant admitted. "That is how I know about these six criminals."

"But they aren't criminals. They were each found not guilty by juries of their peers," Pat insisted.

"The juries were wrong!" Peeved screamed. He jumped toward Pat, who rushed out of the billiard room, slamming the sliding doors behind her on her pursuer's nose. Pat raced across the drawing room to the French doors. Locked! Behind her, the sliding doors opened and Peeved erupted, holding his nose. He leaped toward Pat, and she pushed a heavy suit of armor in his path. He crashed into it with the force of a downfield block.

Pat dashed into the hallway, only to find the front door was locked, too. The key was missing. Pat overturned chairs rushing away from Peeved and then ducked into a dark cloakroom. She stopped, breathing heavily, and listened for the lunatic's footfalls.

But the next attack came from behind her, where a sliding panel slowly, noiselessly opened in the wall. A hand was clamped over the mouth of the unsuspecting mathematician, and she was dragged from the room, the panel slamming shut behind her.

I'm done for, Pat thought, *but I'll go down fighting*. She turned, ready to do battle with her assailant, and stared into the eyes of . . . her partner.

"George Frankly, where in the world . . . ?"

"Are you okay, Pard?" George asked.

"Just peachy," Pat sputtered. "Where *were* you?"

"In these passageways. Pat, they run all through the house. It's like a honeycomb, and practically every room is accessible by secret passage," he said, rubbing his hands in

boyish glee. "Peeved left a passageway open in his room."

"Great," Pat said sarcastically. "You're off admiring architecture while some mathematics-hating court steno is trying to do me in."

"You were safe," George said. "I've been listening."

"Listening?" Pat said.

"Come on." George slipped away into the darkness.

Pat followed her partner as he led her through the dark passageway.

"This whole house is wired for sound," George said. "Hidden speakers and monitors are mounted all over the place. Did you notice something peculiar about the screams we kept hearing?"

Pat shook her head.

"I did," George said, "but I couldn't put my finger on it. There were really just two . . . a man's scream and a woman's scream. The same ones over and over. They were recorded on a tape player that was connected to a computer. It was programmed where and when to go off. Peeved controlled all of it."

"You mean," Pat asked, "when I heard a man scream upstairs . . . "

"Yes, and I heard a woman scream downstairs—the tape was programmed to do that. Pretty slick, huh?" George said. He pointed to a giant electronic console mounted on the passageway wall.

Pat looked at its switches, buttons, gauges, and meters. "I'm impressed," she said. "But have you found the others?"

"No," George admitted, "but I've heard them and they're okay. Let's see if we can find them."

They examined the labels on the console until they found a switch marked "Dungeon."

"What do you want to bet that's the one?" George offered.

"Charming," Pat said and hit the switch. From one of the console's speakers, they heard Peeved's voice.

"Hear ye, hear ye, hear ye . . . the Court of Last Resort is now in session. All who have business in front of me shall now rise. Justice will be done!"

"I guess he got tired of chasing you," George said, chuckling.

"I was playing hard to get," Pat admitted. "But wait, if Peeved is behind this, who knocked him out?"

"He did it himself," George said, "to throw us off."

Peeved's voice blasted from the speakers. "The case of the People vs. Amanda Wine, accused of slandering Grover Cleveland, the twenty-second president of the United States."

They heard Amanda's voice, in shrill protestation. "I have already been tried and found innocent. Besides, Grover Cleveland was also the twenty-fourth president of the country. He won twice."

"Yes! You slandered a man *twice* elected president of this great land by lying about him," Peeved thundered.

"I didn't lie," Amanda snapped back. "I said he was the only man to win the popular vote and yet lose a presidential election."

"That's the lie. A winner *cannot* be a loser," Peeved growled, gaveling for order.

"I'll try to explain it to you," Ms. Wine said. "In 1888 Cleveland ran for president against Benjamin Harrison. Cleveland got 5,540,050 popular votes and Harrison got only 5,444,337. Yet Harrison won the election because he got 233 *electoral* votes to Cleveland's 168."

Peeved exploded. "Mathematical trickery! You are guilty as charged and sentenced to spend ten years at Wit's End."

Pat shook her head at the console. "See what we're up against?" she said to George.

George nodded. "A real Math-phobe," he said.

The two intrepid mathematicians pushed along the passageway as the sound from the kangaroo court continued broadcasting through the speaker system.

"And you, Colonel Wiggston, are guilty of stealing ten thousand silver coins," Peeved continued.

"I was found not guilty, you ninny. I proved mathematically that the weight of ten thousand silver coins could not possibly be carried by one man," the Colonel said in his defense.

"And I proved through a simple comparison of distance, rate, and time that I couldn't have robbed that bank," Wally whispered.

Peeved erupted, "Mathematics again . . . trickery and deceit. I'll have none of it. I find you both guilty and you will spend the next seven years at Wit's End."

"Doing what?" Wiggston demanded.

"Doing whatever I tell you to do," harangued the demented judge. "I think it is becoming clear, my dear criminals, that we live in a land of laws, not of mathematics. You'll never trick anybody with math again."

"We didn't trick anybody, man," Miles Toogo said. "Mathematics helped us tell the truth."

"Truth? Ha!" Peeved just laughed.

"Yeah, the truth, man," Miles said. "Take my case. I was accused of stealing some priceless Stradivarius violin from a museum."

"And you were guilty!" Peeved's voice thundered. Pat and George thought they were getting closer.

"No, man," Miles said. "We were in the middle of a set when it happened. I left the stage to clean my spit valve while the lead was grabbing a solo."

"And that's when you committed the crime," Peeved said.

"No. I proved mathematically that at the tempo that cat was playing, there was no time for me to get to the museum and back before my solo, man."

Peeved just snorted.

Sally's voice echoed from the speakers next. "And I used math to prove that the skid marks left by my car indicated I was going the legal speed limit. I didn't cause that auto accident."

"Lies, all lies," Peeved mumbled.

"And what about me?" Kitty chimed in. "I proved that the money from those fur thefts couldn't have been the source of the income I was making." She laughed. "There was a lot more in my bank account than I could get fencing stolen furs. I mean, the going rate for fenced furs was only ten percent of the real value."

"I don't understand any of that," Peeved said in an unhappy voice. "It's all nonsense."

"Did you ever study math in school?" Kitty asked.

"Of course I did," the beleaguered jurist shot back. Then he paused. "Perhaps 'study' is too strong a word," he admitted.

"You didn't do well in math?" Kitty pressed on.

"No, I didn't," Peeved admitted, "and do you know why? Because I couldn't see where I would ever use it in real life."

"You flunked?" the prisoners chorused.

"So what if I did?" Peeved asked. "So what? I now sit as judge and jury of your feeble, math-infected lives."

Pat and George pushed open a door at the bottom of a set of stairs and found themselves looking into a torch-lit dungeon. Peeved, as magistrate, sat at a high desk. He was dressed in a black robe and sported a white horsehair wig. He looked for all the world like a proper English judge. The defendants were locked in a cell.

"George," Pat whispered, "I think I can get around behind Peeved."

"And do what?" her partner asked softly.

"Watch," Pat ordered. She moved away quietly.

The defendants saw Pat slip behind the judge. They began banging on the bars of their cell as a distraction.

"Stop that banging," Peeved ordered. "You've been watching too many prison movies on the telly."

When she was in place behind Peeved, Pat reached around and grabbed the judge's gavel without his spying her. She stuck the handle in the back of Peeved's robe, saying, "All right, Peeved, put up your dukes."

The startled magistrate raised his hands and grabbed for sky. Before Peeved could turn around, George rushed up.

The kidnap victims hooted and cheered. "Peeved, man, the gig is up," Miles said as George and Pat tackled the host of what had become a *real* mystery weekend.

* * *

Later, in the drawing room, the morning sun shone brilliantly through the French doors as George finished tying Peeved to a chair.

"I can't believe you'd go to all this trouble just because you hate math, man," Miles said to Peeved, shaking his head sadly.

"Such a shame," George muttered, "since mathematics is accessible to everyone . . . and it's free."

"It *is* a shame," Pat agreed. She looked sadly at the phony butler. "Especially since you're so good at it."

"Good at math?" Peeved said in disbelief.

"You sure are," George said. "You set up some beautiful mathematical patterns . . . the colors . . . the times . . . the chart. That was brilliant stuff."

"It was?" asked Peeved, looking a bit more chipper. "Really? That was mathematics? I thought math was just adding, subtracting, multiplying, and dividing."

"That's arithmetic," Pat said.

"Arithmetic is just a tiny part of mathematics," George added.

"Well then," Peeved said brightly, "perhaps I should take up the subject again."

"I think you'll have plenty of time to do just that," George said.

"About seven to ten years," Pat added.

The mystery weekenders looked on in wonder as Sherlock and Whatzit exchanged a congratulatory high five.

DUM DE DUM DUM

EPILOGUE

Peeved the Butler was tried in Sullivan County in and for the State of New York and found guilty of a 135.20, kidnapping in the first degree; and a 120.15, impersonating an English judge. He went to state prison where he has learned to love mathematics, and currently advises his fellow inmates on the finer points of butlery.

ACTIVITIES

Pat and George love number games
and patterns, but it's number trickery
like this that drove poor Peeved over
the edge. You can only play this trick
once on a person, because even though
it seems the answer must be different
every time, the answer is always four. Begin by asking your
friend for a number—any number. Tell your friend you can
make it equal four. Then follow the pattern shown below.

EXAMPLE

Write down a number:	**43**
Write it as a word:	***forty-three***
Count the letters:	**10**
Write that new word as a word:	***ten***
Count the letters:	**3**
Write that new word as a word:	***three***
Count the letters:	**5**
Write that new word as a word:	***five***
Count the letters:	**4**
Write that new word as a word:	***four***
Count the letters:	**4**

No matter what number you begin with,
the answer is always four.

DUM DE DUM DUM

WHOSE ROOM?

After the culprit was arrested, the guests decided to stay overnight. They were all assigned new rooms, except for Pat and George, who stayed in their original rooms. In the middle of the night, there was a loud scream. Everyone either hid in a closet or looked out the door. From the following clues, can you figure out who was staying in which room, and which guest was missing?

- Sally insisted on having the green room. She said it was her most flattering color. (She was wrong.)
- From her room, Amanda could see Pat and Sally peering out their doors.
- George and Miles met in the missing guest's closet. All three had connecting closets.
- Wally and Kitty bumped into each other while hiding in their connecting closets.

The grid below should help you figure things out. Mark an X when you know someone can't be in a room and an O when you know which room he or she is in. To start you off, the first clue has already been marked on the chart. Remember, except for Pat and George, the guests are not in their old rooms, so you can cross those possibilities off, too. (Turn the page to see the old room assignments.)

	Red	Orange	Yellow	Green	Blue	Violet
Wally				X		
Wiggins				X		
Kitty				X		
Amanda				X		
Miles				X		
Sally	X	X	X	O	X	X

OLD ROOM ASSIGNMENTS

(Make a copy of this chart. Cross out the old names and write in the new room assignments as you guess them.)

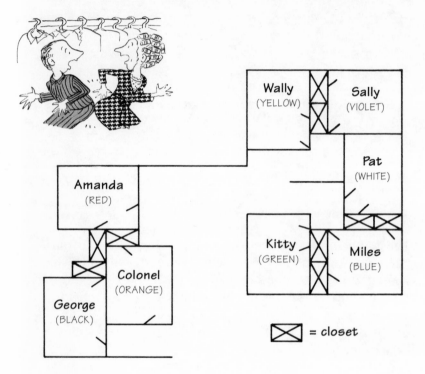

ANSWERS

Whose Room: Sally has the Green Room; Amanda has the Blue Room; Wally has the Violet Room; Kitty has the Yellow Room; Miles has the Orange Room; Wiggins (the missing guest) has the Red Room. Pat and George are still in their old rooms, White and Black.

64